# IRA CRUMB
## Makes a Pretty Good Friend

Or so I've heard...

For the Super Secret Writing Clubbers—N.H.
To my dog, Jack. He makes a pretty good friend—J.H.

# IRA CRUMB
## Makes a Pretty Good Friend

Written by Naseem Hrab & Illustrated by Josh Holinaty

Let's do this!

OWLKIDS BOOKS

# Meet Ira Crumb.
He just moved here.
And he has all the makings
of a pretty good friend.

He's trustworthy.

He's always super helpful.

But it doesn't matter that Ira is trustworthy,
super helpful, and also really fun to be around.
By September, Ira knows he'll only be one thing:
The New Kid.

The New Kid plays alone at recess,

eats alone at lunch,

and walks home alone
at the end of the day.

But Ira's not worried. He has a plan!
He's going to make friends
BEFORE the first day of school.

Ira comes up with an idea —
he'll show everyone how much fun he is.

Maybe the dance off wasn't such a good idea.
But that's ok—Ira can just show everyone
how cool he is.

**School is going to be HORRIBLE.**

**You're Ira, right?**

**I'm Malcolm.**

**Nice to meet you, Malcolm the Sandwich.**

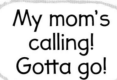 **Malcolm!**

My mom's calling! Gotta go!

 I'm sorry, but I can't let you go.

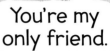 You're my only friend.

 And you're just too delicious.

 **OUCH!**

 I'm sorry, Malcolm!

I'm not Malcolm!

 My name's Phillip!

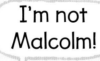

On Ira's first day of school, his dad packs
him a cheesy sandwich with extra pickles,
and Ira walks to school alone.

Well... I dressed like a pirate and asked everyone to come aboard my friend ship.

FRIEND. SHIP.

Heh.

# Best! Idea! Ever!

Owlkids Books acknowledges the financial support of the Canada Council for the Arts, the Ontario Arts Council, the Government of Canada through the Canada Book Fund (CBF) and the Government of Ontario through the Ontario Media Development Corporation's Book Initiative for our publishing activities.

Published in Canada by
Owlkids Books Inc.
10 Lower Spadina Avenue
Toronto, ON M5V 2Z2

Published in the United States by
Owlkids Books Inc.
1700 Fourth Street
Berkeley, CA 94710

Library and Archives Canada Cataloguing in Publication

Hrab, Naseem, author
        Ira Crumb makes a pretty good friend / written by Naseem  Hrab ; illustrated by Josh Holinaty.

ISBN 978-1-77147-171-8 (hardcover)

        I. Holinaty, Josh, illustrator  II. Title.

PS8615.R317I73 2017          jC813.6          C2016-908275-X

Library of Congress Control Number: 2016962478

Edited by: Karen Li and Karen Boersma
Designed by: Danielle Arbour

Manufactured in Dongguan, China, in April 2017, by Toppan Leefung Packaging & Printing (Dongguan) Co., Ltd.
Job #BAYDC38

A          B          C          D          E          F